Helen E. Buckley

SOMEDAY
With My Father

PICTURES BY
Ellen Eagle

Harper & Row, Publishers

Someday With My Father
Text copyright © 1985 by Helen E. Buckley
Illustrations copyright © 1985 by Ellen Eagle
Printed in the U.S.A. All rights reserved.
10 9 8 7 6 5 4 3 2 1
First Edition

Library of Congress Cataloging in Publication Data
Buckley, Helen Elizabeth.
  Someday with my father.

  Summary: A little girl daydreams about the fun she
and her father will have once she is well.
  1. Children's stories, American. [1. Fathers and
daughters—Fiction. 2. Sick—Fiction] I. Eagle,
Ellen, ill. II. Title.
PZ7.B882Sp 1985   [E]   85-42637
ISBN 0-06-020877-5
ISBN 0-06-020878-3 (lib. bdg.)

5013639

For Frank and Niesha
H.E.B.

For Gordon and our fathers
E.E.

Someday
I'm going skiing
with my father.
He promised me.

We'll wear our puffy jackets,
our ski caps and mittens,
our slippery ski pants,
and we'll put on
our big boots and long skis.

We'll take the chair lift
to the top of a big hill

and go whooshing down.
And when we get
to the bottom
my father will say:

"What a good skier you are!"

Someday
I'm going fishing
with my father.
He promised me.

We'll wear our high rubber boots,
and our jackets with all the pockets.
In the pockets we'll put
little silver spinners,
some extra fishline,
and maybe a couple of worms.

We'll take
our fishing poles
and net,

and we'll wade
into the water
and cast our
lines.

I will catch
the biggest fish,
and my father
will say:

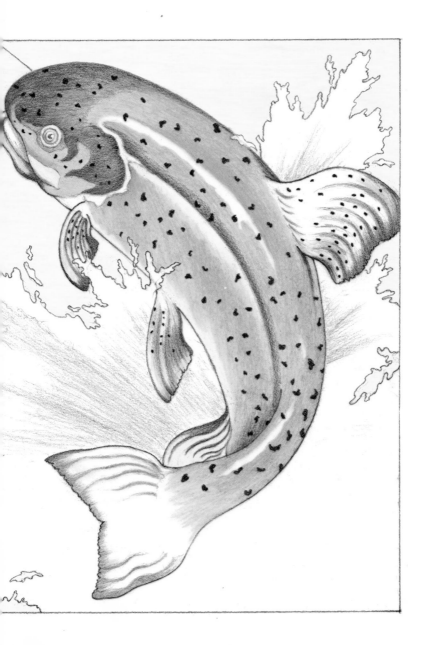

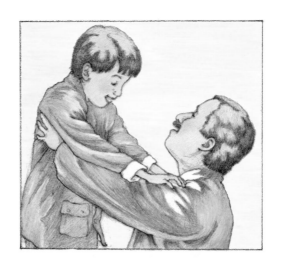

"What a good fisherman you are!"

Someday
I'm going sailing
with my father.
He promised me.

We'll wear our
swimsuits and life jackets,
and our boat shoes with the ripples
on the bottom.
I'll help my father
push the boat into the water.

Then I'll climb on board
and hold the tiller steady
while my father tightens the lines.

When the wind catches the sail,
and we go skimming along,
my father will say:

"What a good sailor you are!"

Someday
I'm going hiking
with my father.
He promised me.

We'll wear our lace-up boots
and warm sweaters,
and we'll take our camera
and put sandwiches and apples
in my backpack.

Then we'll walk
into the woods to the pond
where the wild geese are.

We'll sit on a rock and be very quiet
and watch them.
And maybe we'll take their picture.
After we have our lunch
we'll pick up the apple cores
and leave all our crumbs for the birds.
And my father will say:

"What a good hiker you are!"

Someday
my father and I
will do all these things.

Someday, when my cast comes off.

But right now
he'll sit by my bed
and read to me.
And when he is finished
I will say:
"What a good reader you are!"

And he will laugh
and give me a hug.